facts

Simple Machines to the Rescue

Levers
to the Rescue

by Sharon Thales

Consultant:
Louis A. Bloomfield, PhD
Professor of Physics
University of Virginia
Charlottesville, Virginia

Capstone *press*®

Mankato, Minnesota

First Facts is published by Capstone Press,
151 Good Counsel Drive, P.O. Box 669, Mankato, Minnesota 56002.
www.capstonepress.com

Library of Congress Cataloging-in-Publication Data
Thales, Sharon.
    Levers to the rescue / Sharon Thales.
    p. cm.—(First facts. Simple machines to the rescue)
    Summary: "Describes levers, including what they are, how they work, past uses, and
common uses of these simple machines today"—Provided by publisher.
    Includes bibliographical references and index.
    ISBN-13: 978-0-7368-6747-4 (hardcover)
    ISBN-10: 0-7368-6747-3 (hardcover)
    1. Levers—Juvenile literature. I. Title. II. Series.
TJ147.T43 2007
621.8—dc22   2006021501

Editorial Credits
Becky Viaene, editor; Thomas Emery, designer; Jo Miller, photo researcher/photo editor

Photo Credits
Capstone Press/Karon Dubke, 6, 10, 13, 18–19, 21 (all); TJ Thoraldson
    Digital Photography, cover
Corbis/Bettmann, 20; Gianni Dagli Orti, 8–9
Photo Courtesy of Louis A. Bloomfield, 12
Shutterstock/Anita Patterson Peppers, 17
UNICORN Stock Photos/Martha McBride, 5; Robert W. Ginn, 14–15

072010
5843VMI

Table of Contents

A Helpful Lever

You want to jump in a big pile of leaves. Making the pile with your hands will take a long time. How can you do the job faster?

Lever to the rescue!

Grab a rake. A rake is a **lever**. Pull the rake along the ground. The rake makes it easier to move leaves into a pile.

fulcrum

effort

load

Work It

A lever is a **simple machine**. Simple machines have one or no moving parts. Machines are used to make **work** easier. Work is using a **force** to move an object.

People use levers to lift items. A lever is a bar that turns on a resting point called a **fulcrum**. You can apply force, called **effort,** to a bar. The bar turns on the fulcrum and moves a **load**.

Lever Fact

Not sure what a lever looks like? Many levers are long straight bars that have handles.

A Lever in Time

Before levers were used, boats were hard to move. People tried moving boats by paddling with their hands. They needed a quicker way to move boats.

Lever to the rescue!

People tried paddling with long flat sticks called oars. These levers made it easier to move boats faster.

9

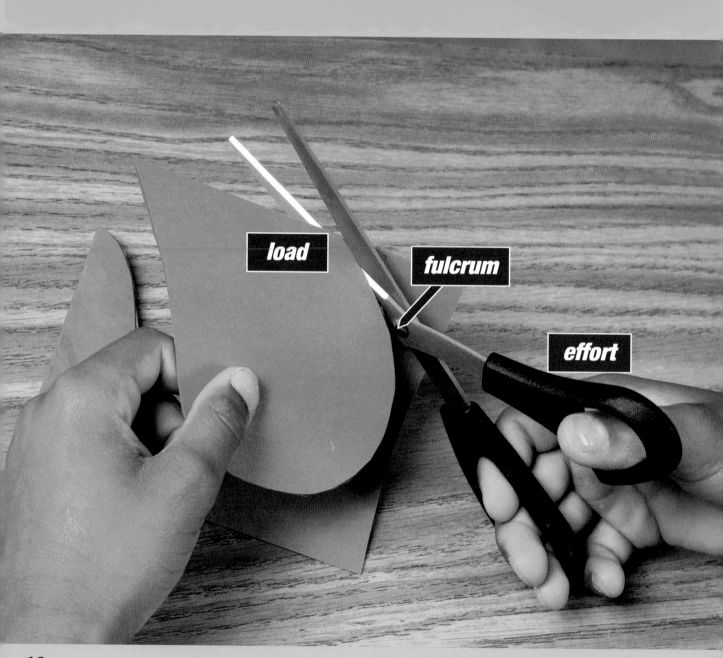

First-Class Levers: Load-Fulcrum-Effort

Levers are sorted into three classes. The classes are based on the location of the fulcrum, effort, and load.

First-class levers have the fulcrum between the load and the effort. Scissors are first-class levers that help you cut out valentines for friends. A seesaw is also a first-class lever.

Lever Fact

The farther it is between the fulcrum and the effort, the less force you need to do work.

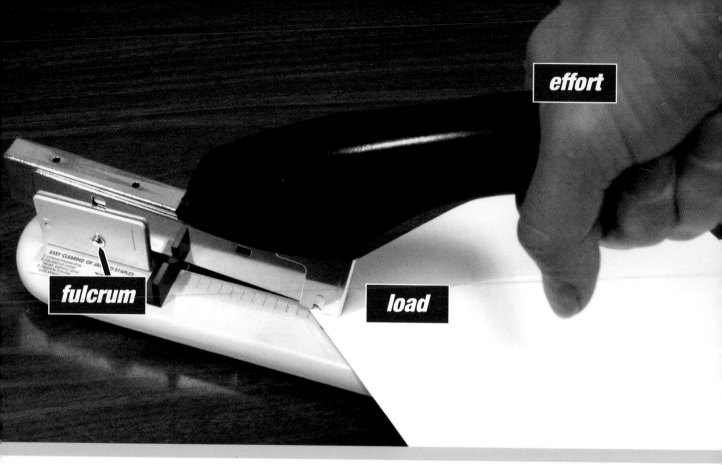

effort

fulcrum

load

Second-Class Levers: Fulcrum-Load-Effort

Second-class levers have the load between the fulcrum and the effort. Want to staple papers or crack some nuts? Second-class levers will save the day!

Third-Class Levers: Load-Effort-Fulcrum

Third-class levers have the effort between the load and the fulcrum. To hit a home run or score a hockey goal, you'll need a third-class lever.

load

effort

fulcrum

What Would We Do Without Levers?

Levers come to our rescue every day. Squeezing two levers together helps people grip things their fingers can't. Your dad uses tongs to take sizzling hotdogs off the grill.

Lever Fact

Tweezers are levers that help people pick up and grip small items. Jewelers use special tweezers to pick up tiny diamonds.

Working Together

A wheelbarrow is a **complex machine**. It is made of several simple machines. To use a wheelbarrow, pull up on the handles. They are second-class levers.

Next, push the wheelbarrow forward to turn the wheel and axle. The fulcrum is where the handles meet the wheel and axle.

Lever Buddies

Six kinds of simple machines combine to make almost every machine there is.

- **Inclined plane**–a slanting surface that is used to move objects to different levels

- **Lever**–a bar that turns on a resting point and is used to lift items

- **Pulley**–a grooved wheel turned by a rope, belt, or chain that often moves heavy objects

- **Screw**–an inclined plane wrapped around a post that usually holds objects together

- **Wedge**–an inclined plane that moves to split things apart or push them together

- **Wheel and axle**–a wheel that turns around a bar to move objects

Levers

Wheel and Axle

Levers Everywhere

Levers are everywhere! Your toothbrush is a lever. Forks and chopsticks are levers too. Working alone or with other simple machines, levers come to the rescue every day.

An ancient Greek scientist named
Archimedes was the first person
to explain how levers do work. He
said, "Give me a firm place to stand,
and I'll move the earth." Wow. What
would he have used for a fulcrum?

Hands On: Working with a Lever

What You Need

heavy book, unsharpened pencil, eraser

What You Do

1. Place the book flat on a table.
2. Put one edge of the book on top of the eraser end of the pencil. Hide about 1 inch (2.5 centimeters) of the pencil under the book.
3. Lift the other end of the pencil and place the eraser underneath about halfway along the pencil. One end of the pencil is now under the book and one end is sticking out into the air.
4. Push down on the pencil end that sticks out. Can you lift the book? What happens when you move the eraser closer to your hand or closer to the book?

The pencil and eraser worked as a lever to lift the book. When you pushed down on the pencil, you applied force to the lever. The closer you move the eraser to the book, the easier it is to lift the book.

Glossary

complex machine (KOM-pleks muh-SHEEN)—a machine made of two or more simple machines

effort (EF-urt)—the force you apply to a lever to move an object

force (FORSS)—a push or a pull

fulcrum (FUL-kruhm)—the resting point where a lever bar turns

lever (LEV-ur)—a bar that turns on a resting point called a fulcrum and is used to lift items

load (LOHD)—the object that moves when a force is applied

simple machine (SIM-puhl muh-SHEEN)—a tool with one or no moving parts that moves an object when you push or pull; levers are simple machines.

work (WURK)—when a force moves an object

Read More

Dahl, Michael. *Scoop, Seesaw, and Raise: A Book about Levers.* Amazing Science. Minneapolis: Picture Window Books, 2005.

Oxlade, Chris. *Levers.* Useful Machines. Chicago: Heinemann Library, 2003.

Tiner, John Hudson. *Levers.* Simple Machines. North Mankato, Minn.: Smart Apple Media, 2003.

Internet Sites

FactHound offers a safe, fun way to find Internet sites related to this book. All of the sites on FactHound have been researched by our staff.

Here's how:

1. Visit *www.facthound.com*

2. Choose your grade level.

3. Type in this book ID **0736867473** for age-appropriate sites. You may also browse subjects by clicking on letters, or by clicking on pictures and words.

4. Click on the **Fetch It** button.

FactHound will fetch the best sites for you!

Index